THE TRUTH ABOUT COUSIN ERNIE'S HEAD

BY MATTHEW McELLIGOTT

Grandma

Uncle Vic

Aunt Helen

Uncle Max

Aunt Edith

Mom

Uncle Ogden

Uncle Klaus

Dad

SIMON & SCHUSTER BOOKS FOR YOUNG READERS

SIMON & SCHUSTER BOOKS FOR YOUNG READERS
An imprint of Simon & Schuster Children's Publishing Division
1230 Avenue of the Americas, New York, New York 10020

Book design by Anahid Hamparian
The text for this book is set in 15-point ITC Quorum
The illustrations are rendered in water-color pencil, water-color, and digital prints
Printed and bound in Hong Kong by South China Printing Co.(1988) Ltd.
First Edition
10 9 8 7 6 5 4 3 2 1
Library of Congress Cataloging-in-Publication Data
McElligott, Matthew.
The truth about Cousin Ernie's head / by Matthew McElligott. — 1st ed.
p.   cm.
Summary: A colorful family's Thanksgiving arguments are ended by
the viewing of an old home movie, which seems to leave no topics for further discussion.
[1. Family life—Fiction. 2. Thanksgiving Day—Fiction.] I. Title
PZ7.M478448Tr 1996
[E]—dc20 95-21743
ISBN 0-689-80179-3

FOR CHRISTY

L AST YEAR, AS USUAL,
we went to my grandmother's house for
Thanksgiving dinner. I didn't really want to go.
There's always a big argument.

Most of my family was there.

Uncle Klaus flew in from Bangladesh.

Aunt Edith, Uncle Vic, and Uncle Ogden took the train up from Florida.

Aunt Helen and Uncle Max rode a bicycle down from Alaska.

"It took us almost a month, but it was worth it," said Uncle Max.

The adults talked all through dinner.

"I'm learning yoga," said Uncle Klaus.

"I ate an airplane, tires and all," said Aunt Edith.

"There's nothing like a good airplane," Uncle Max agreed. "Remember the time that airplane landed on Cousin Ernie's head?"

"Max, you know very well it wasn't an airplane," said Aunt Helen. "It was a buzzard."

"Pardon me," said Uncle Ogden, softly, "but it wasn't an airplane or a buzzard. I remember quite clearly. It was Mrs. Halusa from next door. She was bringing us a casserole."

Soon everyone was arguing about Cousin Ernie's head.

My family is crazy like that. Even though they grew up together, they all remember things differently. One year they spent the entire day arguing about what happened to my dad's hat. Another year they got in a big fight over Aunt Helen and the barbecue.

Last year, while everyone was downstairs arguing, I went up to the attic to find some peace and quiet.

I found an old movie.

I brought it down and showed it to my grandmother.

"I haven't seen that in years," she said. "Your grandfather had a little movie camera. He was always taking pictures of the family. That's one of his movies."

Everyone wanted to watch it. I helped clear the table. My grandmother found the projector and set it up. Uncle Klaus turned out the lights.

It wasn't like any movie I had ever seen. It was just a bunch of short scenes of my family when they were younger. The movie was blurry and hard to look at, and parts of it were upside down.

At first, I hated it. Then I began to notice something. The adults began to notice it, too. Hidden within those scenes were the answers to all the silly arguments my family had been having for years! Suddenly, everyone began to pay very close attention. Watching the movie we learned that . . .

The unicycle bandit stole my dad's hat.

Aunt Helen WAS at the liver and onions barbecue.

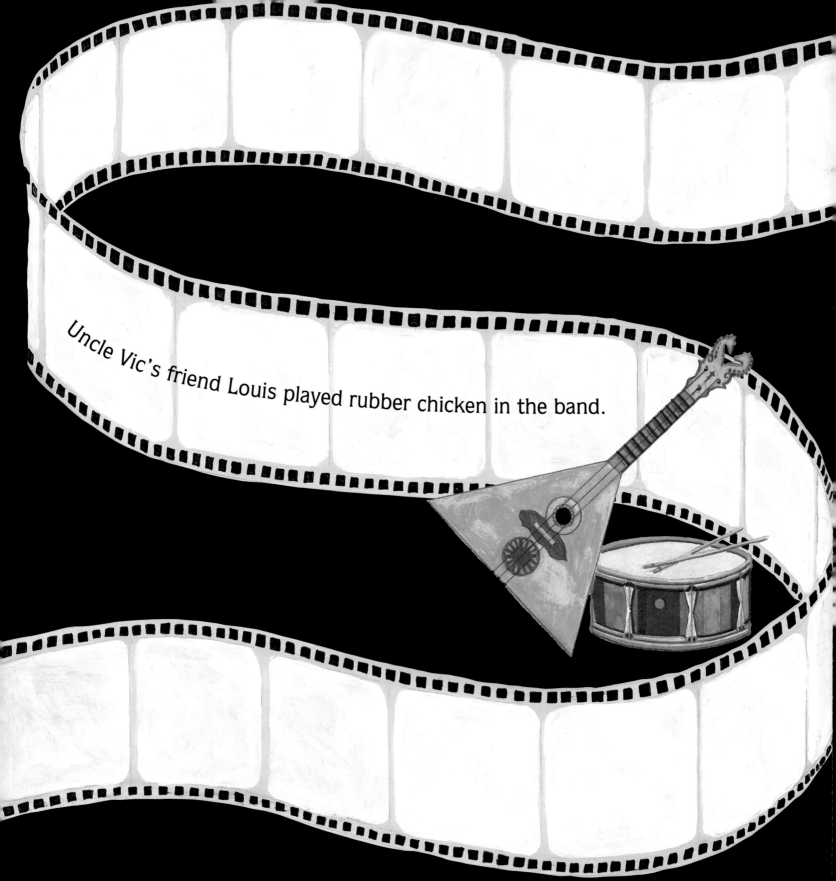

Uncle Vic's friend Louis played rubber chicken in the band.

Aunt Edith kept toads in the trunk for emergencies.

It was not an airplane.

It was not a buzzard.

It was Mrs. Halusa and her casserole that landed on Cousin Ernie's head.

When the movie finished, everyone was very quiet.

"Well, that settles it," said Uncle Klaus.
"It certainly does," said Aunt Edith.

"Yes," said my dad, "that certainly settles it."

It was eerie, and kind of sad. My family, normally the loudest in the neighborhood, suddenly had nothing left to argue about. No one spoke much the rest of the day. By seven-thirty, everyone had gone home. It was the shortest Thanksgiving ever.

This year, as usual, we returned to my grandmother's for Thanksgiving dinner. It wasn't the same. The adults looked kind of nervous. Instead of having loud, crazy conversations, everyone pretended to watch television. I knew they were faking. They hate wrestling.

My grandmother noticed it, too. Our family looked like deflated balloons. The longer we watched, the less they moved. Something had to be done before they completely dried up.

I had an idea. I whispered it to my grandmother.

"I suppose you're right," she sighed. "With nincompoops like these, I'm afraid it's the only answer."

"Everyone, listen to me," she said, clearing her throat.

Everyone turned and listened.
"Remember that movie? I lost it."
"What?" said Uncle Max.
"What?" said Aunt Edith.
"What?" said everyone else at the same time.
"I lost it," said my grandmother, "or I threw it away, or it blew up, or something. Anyway, it's gone.

"That's a shame," said my dad.

"Yes," said Aunt Edith. "But at least we all got to see it."

"Yes," said Uncle Klaus. "At least we all know what really happened."

"No more fights about Mrs. Halusa and Cousin Ernie's head," said Uncle Ogden, softly.

"Again with Mrs. Halusa?" said Aunt Helen. "I thought we settled this. It was a buzzard that landed on his head."

"It was an airplane, you ninnies!" shouted Uncle Max. "Airplane, airplane, airplane!"

Within minutes my family was normal again. They argued the rest of the day and into the night.

They can argue all they want. I don't mind. I know what really happened.